Spirulina and the
Lost Whale

Join Spirulina and her sisters for more mermaid adventures:

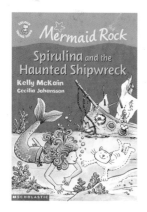

And why not try some other Colour Young Hippo titles too!

Beetle and Friends

Mermaid Rock

Millie and Bombassa

Sherlock Hound

Creepy Crawlies

Fat Alphie and Charlie the Wimp

Tales from Whispery Wood

Buster Gutt

Spirulina and the Lost Whale

Kelly McKain
illustrated by Cecilia Johansson

SCHOLASTIC

For my mummy

Scholastic Children's Books,
Commonwealth House, 1-19 New Oxford Street,
London, WC1A 1NU, UK
a division of Scholastic Ltd
London ~ New York ~ Toronto ~ Sydney ~ Auckland
Mexico City ~ New Delhi ~ Hong Kong

First published by Scholastic Ltd, 2005

ISBN 0 439 95942 X

Printed and bound by Tien Wah Press Pte. Ltd, Singapore

10 9 8 7 6 5 4 3 2 1

I'm a mermaid, a beautiful mermaid, sitting on a rock looking pretty!

It was a beautiful day on Mermaid Rock – just right for playing on the beach or splashing in the sea. But poor Spirulina had no one to play with. You see, Coralie and Shelle were sitting still, combing their hair and singing mermaid songs.

Spirulina joined in, singing the wrong words on purpose. Shelle squealed and put her hands over her ears.

"That's not how the song goes!" she cried.

What a pity, I'm so bored, bored, bored!

"Well, I *am* bored, bored, bored," Spirulina huffed. "Why won't you play with me? I want to have some fun!"

"But having fun messes up our hair!" said Shelle.

Just then, a shoal of silver fish swam by,
flashing and glimmering in the water.

"Those little fish will be much more fun
than you," said Spirulina,
scowling at her sisters.
"I'm going to
play with *them*
instead!"

With that, she dived off Mermaid Rock
and disappeared under the foamy waves.

"Mind you don't get caught in a net!" called Coralie. "There are fishing boats about!"

But Spirulina didn't hear her. She was already far out to sea, following the little fish.

When Spirulina arrived at the seaweed stones, where the little fish played, she got a big surprise. A baby whale was there too!

"Hello, I'm Spirulina," said Spirulina.

"I'm Splosh," said the baby whale. "I followed the little fish. Come on, let's play!"

The little fish let Spirulina and Splosh join in all their games.

They played Sleeping Lionfish…

…Fish and Shark…

...and Pin the Seaweed on the Piranha.

They had so much fun! But then Splosh stopped playing.

"What's wrong?" asked Spirulina.

Splosh looked up and down. Then he started to cry. "I can't see my mummy," he wailed. "I'm lost!"

☆ Chapter Two ☆

Spirulina put her arm round Splosh. "Don't worry," she said. "We'll find your mummy. Where were you before you followed the little fish?"

"I can't remember," Splosh sobbed. "And I forgot to tell her where I was going!"

"That's okay, I'll think of something," Spirulina promised. She thought really, really hard until…

"I've got it!" she cried. "We'll sing the whale song!"

"What's that?" asked the littlest little fish.

"It's a special song that whales can hear from far away," Spirulina explained. "Splosh's mummy will hear us and come and find him."

"Hooray!" cheered Splosh.

So they all sang the whale song.

Whales, whales, out at sea, hear this song and come to me!

Then they waited … but Splosh's mummy didn't come.

"Once more!" shouted Spirulina. "As loud as you can!" Everybody sang until they were about to burst.

13

Suddenly, a huge
shape came gliding
towards them.

"Look, Mummy's coming!" cried
Splosh in delight.
The little fish all cheered and
hugged Spirulina.

But wait … something was wrong.

"That's not my mummy!" Splosh gasped.
"That's a fishing
boat!"

A fishing net was trailing behind the boat.
Everyone screamed and tried to swim
away, but it was too late.
The net scooped them
all up!

"Quick, everyone! Wriggle!" called the littlest little fish.

All the little fish wriggled and wriggled until they had wriggled right out of the net.

Spirulina and Splosh wriggled as well, but they were just *too* big. In desperation, they beat their tails up and down.

The fishing boat rocked from side to side and the net started to fray.

"We're nearly free!" cried Spirulina. "Keep going!"

The threads of the net were just about to break when…

"Argghhhhhh!" they screamed.

The net was wrenched out of the water.

They were trapped!

☆ Chapter Three ☆

When the three fishermen saw the net, they were amazed.

"Cor blimey, a real live mermaid and a baby whale!" gasped one.

"Let us go!" shouted Spirulina, still struggling.

The big fisherman leaped
forward and started to
untangle the net. He
had red hair just
like Spirulina. She
grinned at him
and he grinned back.

"Leave her there, Softy Bill!" shouted one
of the other fishermen as his mate put down
the anchor. "People will pay a lot of money
to see a mermaid. We'll show
her at fairs. We'll make a
fortune, won't we,
Fastnet?"

"Aye, Fisher," said
Fastnet. "She'll only
need a tiny tank.
Or even just a
large bucket."

Spirulina
shuddered.

"You can't do that to me!" she shouted.

"Oh yes we can," said Fisher and Fastnet,
chuckling. They lowered the net on to the

deck and

pulled

Splosh

out.

Spirulina's heart leaped. "At least they're letting you go, Splosh!" she cried. But they didn't. Instead they tied him down to the deck with a strong rope.

"That'll stop you rocking the boat," snapped Fisher.

"Oh, please don't do that!" bellowed Softy Bill. "He's only a baby!"

"Shut up, you big pudding," snarled Fastnet. Softy Bill hung his head.

Then Fisher and Fastnet tied Spirulina to the boat's mast. "You'd better stay put too, mermaid – or else," sneered Fastnet.

Spirulina was furious. But she knew she had to escape and save Splosh.

"Come on, Fisher. Let's go below deck to find something to put that pesky mermaid in," said Fastnet. "Softy Bill, you guard her."

Softy Bill came and stood next to Spirulina. Spirulina thought for a moment.

Then she smiled at him. "You're not a softy," she said. "I think you could be

quite brave, if you tried." Softy Bill blinked at her. "Really?" he asked. Spirulina nodded. "In fact, you could be brave right now, by helping me to escape."

For a moment, Spirulina thought Softy
Bill was going to help. But then, Fisher and
Fastnet reappeared on deck with a large
bucket. Softy Bill cast a nervous glance at
them. "I can't,"
he mumbled.
"I'll get
into
trouble."
   "Well, at least
help poor Splosh," said
Spirulina quickly. "Whales
don't like being out of the ocean.
He needs to stay nice and wet. You could
use that bucket to pour water over him."

"Oi, Softy, stop chinwagging with that mermaid and make us some fish paste sandwiches!" shouted Fastnet.

Softy Bill gave Spirulina a sad look and scurried away. But before he went below deck he sneakily poured a bucket of water over Splosh. Spirulina smiled to herself and started planning her escape.

☆ Chapter Four ☆

Splishity-splash! Splishity-splash!

What was that? Spirulina listened hard...

The little fish! They must be swimming around next to the boat.

"Pssst! Little fish!" hissed Spirulina. "Is that you?"

"Yes," said the littlest little fish.

"Oh good," whispered Spirulina. "I need your help. Can you distract Fisher and Fastnet for me?"

"No problem," whispered the littlest little fish. "This will be fun!"

The little fish swam around just out of reach, shouting rude things and blowing raspberries at Fisher and Fastnet.

"Grrr," growled Fisher. "We'll make you lot into fish paste!"

Spirulina set to work.
First she wriggled
her hand down
to her tool belt.
Then she grabbed
her saw and started
cutting through the net.
It took a long time but, finally, she
freed herself and crept across the deck.

"Yay!" cried Splosh. "I'm saved!"

"Shhh!" hissed Spirulina.
"They'll hear us!"

Spirulina started to saw through Splosh's ropes, but they were just too thick.

"Oh no!" wailed Splosh, starting to cry again.

Splosh's crying made Fisher and Fastnet turn around. "Oi! Stop that!" they shouted, lumbering down the deck after Spirulina. Fisher grabbed her but she slid through his fingers and dived into the sea.

"Follow me!" she called to the little fish.
"Back to the seaweed stones!"

When they arrived, Spirulina found the
piranha. "Please can you help us?"
she asked, very politely.

"No way!"
grumbled the
piranha. "Not
after you tried
to pin the
seaweed on me!"
He snarled and snapped his teeth at her.

Spirulina leaped backwards. "Oh, please don't bite me!" she cried. "I'm sorry about the seaweed. We really, really need you."

"Really?" said the piranha, peering at her.

"Oh yes," said Spirulina. "We need you because you're brilliant at biting."

The piranha looked pleased. "I *am* brilliant at biting," he said. "Okay, what do you want me to do?"

Once Spirulina had explained, they all
swam back to the fishing boat.

Spirulina climbed up the side with the
piranha hidden in her tangled hair.

Softy Bill was still below deck but Fisher and Fastnet were leaning over the side of the boat raising the anchor. The little fish swam over to them and started to shout rude things.

Spirulina took a deep breath, crossed her fingers for luck and hurried over to Splosh.

☆ Chapter Five ☆

Chomp! Chomp! Chomp!

The piranha's teeth flashed like steel. In two seconds flat, he had bitten through Splosh's ropes!

"Wow! Thanks!" whispered Spirulina.

"My pleasure," said the piranha, flipping himself back up into her hair.

Spirulina was just trying to push Splosh over the side of the boat when Fisher spotted her.

"Oh no you don't!" he snarled, running over and grabbing her. Spirulina fought back with all her might but this time she couldn't get away.

Splosh began to thrash around, making the boat rock … until Fastnet dashed over and sat on him.

They were well and truly caught. But Spirulina refused to give up. "Quick, everyone, sing the whale song!" she cried.

She started to sing and the little fish and Splosh joined in.

Whales, whales, out at sea, hear this song and come to me!

"Be quiet!" demanded Fisher. He reached out to put his hand over Spirulina's mouth.

"Oooooowwwww!" he screamed. The piranha had swung down from Spirulina's hair and chomped on his hand.

Fisher staggered backwards
and Spirulina was free.

"Wow, thanks again!"
she gasped.

"No problem!" said
the piranha proudly.

"Keep singing,
everyone!" cried Spirulina.

Just then, Softy Bill appeared on deck with
a plate of sandwiches. He blinked at them in
amazement.

"Help us, Softy Bill!" Spirulina begged.
But Softy Bill shook his head. "I – I –
I'm not allowed," he mumbled
nervously,
glancing at Fisher
and Fastnet.

"Oh please," she cried. But Softy Bill stayed silent.

They sang as loudly as they could. But Splosh's mummy *still* didn't come. Spirulina's heart sank. It was hopeless … but then…

A booming voice joined in. It was Softy Bill!

"Oi, Softy, stop that right now!" ordered Fastnet, but Softy Bill just clenched his fists and kept on singing. His bellowing voice boomed through the air.

Suddenly there was a rumbling and a rocking and a roaring. The boat began to shake.

"Oh-er!" said Fisher.

"Oh-eck!" said Fastnet.

WHOOSH!

The boat was tossed right up out of the water. Spirulina and Splosh and the fishermen flew through the air.

"Arrggghhhh!"

SPLASH!

They crashed into the sea. Splosh's mummy had come at last.

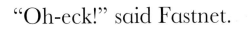

"You found me!" cried Splosh, swimming to her side.

"I heard the whale song," she said, hugging him tight. "Oh, you gave me such a fright! I've been looking everywhere for you! Never *ever* swim off on your own again!"

"Don't worry, I won't!" promised Splosh.

The three fishermen thrashed about helplessly in the water. Spirulina rescued Softy Bill and put him back in the fishing boat.

"Help! Help! Please save us too, kind mermaid!" spluttered Fisher.

Spirulina scowled. "Why should I?"

"We'll change our ways!" gurgled Fastnet.

"I'll make sure they do," called Softy Bill. "I'm taking charge of this boat. And from now on, my name is Brave Bill. Got that?"

"Yes, Captain Brave Bill," cried Fisher.

So Spirulina rescued them too.

"Well done, Brave Bill," said Spirulina. "Without your booming voice Splosh's mummy would never have heard us."

Everyone cheered for Brave Bill.

Brave Bill grinned. "Thanks for making me brave," he said. Then he sailed the fishing boat away, waving from the helm.

"Thank you for saving my baby, Spirulina,"
said Splosh's mummy, who was called Splash.

Spirulina blushed. "It wasn't just me," she
insisted. "It was all of us working together."

"Would you like a ride home?" asked Splosh.

"Yes, please!" said Spirulina, beaming.

☆ ☆ ☆

Coralie and Shelle could hardly believe their eyes when Spirulina came riding up to Mermaid Rock on a whale!

"Spirulina's singing saved me from the fishermen," Splosh told them. He thrashed his tail in delight, drenching them all.

"Arghhh!" cried Coralie and Shelle.

"Oops, sorry!" said Splosh.

Spirulina just laughed and shook her tangled hair. "Will you play with us?" she asked.

"Of course we will," said Coralie.

"After all, we can't get any messier!" added Shelle.

They played with Splosh and his mummy until sunset.

Then, tired and happy the three mermaids said goodbye to the two whales. They stood on Mermaid Rock, waving and waving. Soon all they could see were two tails, one big and one little, arching on the horizon. Spirulina smiled to herself and wondered what her next adventure would be.